Dear Parents:

Children learn to read in stages, and all children develop reading skills at different ages. **Ready Readers**™ were created to promote children's interest in reading and to increase their reading skills. **Ready Readers**™ are written on two levels to accommodate children ranging in age from three through eight. These stages are meant to be used only as a guide.

Stage 1: Preschool-Grade 1
Stage 1 books are written in very short, simple sentences with large type. They are perfect for children who are getting ready to read or are just becoming familiar with reading on their own.

Stage 2: Grades 1-3
Stage 2 books have longer sentences and are a bit more complex. They are suitable for children who are able to read but still may need help.

All the **Ready Readers**™ tell varied, easy-to-follow stories and are colorfully illustrated. Reading will be fun, and soon your child will not only be ready, but eager to read.

SAM AND PEPPER'S
TREE HOUSE

Written by Eugene Bradley Coco
Illustrated by Linda Blassingame

Modern Publishing
A Division of Unisystems, Inc.
New York, New York 10022

One day, Sam and Pepper
went for a walk in the woods.

They saw many trees,
with many branches.

Pepper jumped up on one
of the branches.

Sam climbed up to get him.
Then they both sat down
on the branch.

From up high, Sam and Pepper
could see far, far away.
They saw blue lakes
and green hills.

They even felt close to the clouds.

Sam liked sitting in the tree.
So did Pepper.

Sam had an idea.
She told Pepper.

"Woof! Woof!" Pepper barked.

Sam knew it was a good idea.
They were going to build
a tree house.

Sam got the wood.

Pepper fetched the rope.

Pepper got tangled in the rope.

Sam laughed.

Pepper laughed, too.

Then Sam got the nails,
a hammer, a saw,
some paint, and a brush.

Sam sawed the wood very carefully.
Pepper helped paint the sign—
he didn't need a brush!

"Sam and Pepper's Tree House" it read.

Sam nailed the last board in place.

The tree house was done.

Sam and Pepper climbed
into their tree house…

...and smiled.